The Story of
LITTLE OWL

Constance Boyle

Woodbury, New York · London · Toronto · Sydney

First U.S. edition published in 1985 by
Barron's Educational Series, Inc.
© Constance Boyle 1985

This book has been designed and produced
by Aurum Press Ltd., 33 Museum Street,
London WC1A 1LD, England.

All inquiries should be addressed to:
Barron's Educational Series, Inc.
113 Crossways Park Drive
Woodbury, New York 11797

International Standard Book No. 0-8120-5638-8
Library of Congress Catalog Card No.

PRINTED IN BELGIUM
5 6 7 8   9 8 7 6 5 4 3 2 1

This is Little Owl.
He lives in
Wrenlea.

Behind him is the house where he lives
with his family.

There are four in Little Owl's family.
First of all, there is his mother.
She has kind dark eyes and a nice
smile.

She always wears
bright colors.

Then there is his
brother Olly.
Olly is older
than
Little
Owl.

There is always a lot of noise when Olly
is about.

And then there is Daddy.
Daddy is the tallest one in the family.

When he came to
talk to Little Owl
at bedtime, he
was almost
as high
as the
door.

This is a family photograph taken when
Little Owl was still a baby.

Little Owl also has uncles and aunts and cousins.

On his third birthday, Uncle Horace came to supper.
He was carrying a large box.

Little Owl sat on the floor and opened
the box.

Inside was a teddy bear!
Little Owl was very excited.
He loved teddy bears.

Little Owl took Teddy to bed with him that night, and Mommy and Daddy and Olly and Uncle Horace all came in to have a look.

Little Owl enjoyed having a teddy
bear, because when Olly went to
school he still had someone to play
with.
Teddy didn't seem to mind what games
they played.

He didn't even
mind being
bandaged.

Teddy used to go shopping with Little Owl.
When Little Owl got tired of carrying him, Mommy gave him a ride in the shopping basket.

One day, when they got home, Teddy wasn't there. However hard they looked, they couldn't find him anywhere.

When Olly got back from school he helped Little Owl look for Teddy. Olly thought it was all great fun, but Little Owl was sad because Teddy was lost.

One day when Little Owl and his
mother were in the park, they saw an
old lady sitting on a bench.

She was knitting.

Sitting next to her was a teddy bear,
wearing a pink hair-ribbon.

Little Owl stopped and stared in
amazement.
It was Teddy!

But why was he wearing a ribbon?
"Hello, are you looking at my teddy
bear?" asked the old lady. "She's a
present for my little granddaughter and
I'm knitting a cardigan to match her
ribbon."

"Goodness!" said Mommy. "She's just like Little Owl's Teddy! He lost his, though," she added.

The old lady looked worried. "Oh dear, I wonder if this could be yours," she said. "I found her just the other day."

She started to undo the ribbon.

"Oh, no, it isn't ours!" said Mommy.
"Our Teddy looked more cheerful."
So the old lady tied the bow again, and
Little Owl and Mommy went home.

Little Owl couldn't eat his supper. "What's the matter?" asked Mommy. "It WAS Teddy," said Little Owl.

"No, Chick, it wasn't, you know," said Mommy. "Your Teddy had a happy face. Besides, he had a cut on his paw, but the other teddy hadn't. Now, cheer up and have some supper."

"We're going to look at teddy bears," said Mommy, some days later. "I want you to choose one." They saw lots of teddy bears but not one like Teddy.

Next morning, Mommy and Little Owl
went to a rummage sale in the Wrenlea
church hall.
The Scouts had a rummage sale there
every year.

Olly was a Cub
Scout and he had
to go early
to help.

When Little Owl
and Mommy
arrived, Olly
rushed up
excitedly.

"Hey, look what I found! I hid it when
no one was looking."
He dived under the toy booth and
came out with a teddy bear.
It was exactly like Teddy, but it was
pink!

Little Owl laughed. It was so funny to
see a teddy just like his in that color.
Mommy saw him laughing.
"Thank GOODNESS!" she thought.

She paid for the pink teddy, and took it
from Olly.

"You don't WANT it, do you?" asked
Olly. "Pink teddies are awful!"
"Well, I know someone who likes it,"
said Mommy, smiling at Little Owl.
He couldn't disappoint her.
"Yes, it's like Teddy," he said bravely.

Little Owl took the pink teddy
shopping and played games with it, just
like he used to do with Teddy.
But it wasn't the same. The pink teddy
didn't enjoy things the way Teddy had,
and Little Owl didn't know what name
to call it.

Little Owl
still missed
Teddy.

"Come on, let's go for a walk,"
Mommy said one day. "Bring your
teddy. You both look as if you need
some fresh air!"

They went a way they hadn't been
before. Little Owl got stuck climbing a
fence, and Mommy had to help him
over.

The path went round the edge of a field and through a little wood.

"Look!" said Little Owl. "What pretty cottages!" exclaimed Mommy.

There was a seat just below them,
facing the cottages.
Little Owl wanted to sit down and have
a rest.

Just then, a little
girl with a doll
carriage came out
of one of the
cottages.
She came over,
and stared at the
pink teddy.

"I've got one,
too," she said,
and lifted a teddy
out of the
carriage.
It was Teddy!
The REAL Teddy!

Little Owl didn't know what to do.
Then suddenly he noticed all the pink
things the little girl had. Even the doll
carriage was pink. He had an idea.

"Do you like pink?" asked Little Owl.
The little girl nodded.
"Would you like my pink teddy?"
She nodded again, beaming.
"Er... can I have yours?"
She hesitated, looking at Teddy, then
gave him to Little Owl.

At that moment, who should come out
of the cottage but the old lady they had
met in the park.
Mommy tried to explain about Teddy.

"Well, the little fellow was right!" said the old lady. "And the teddy DID have a torn paw! I mended it."

The pink teddy looked lovely in the pink clothes. The little girl called her "Rose."

"I still can't understand it," said Mommy on the way home.

"Teddy didn't look himself at all when we saw him in the park."

"He doesn't like pink ribbons, that's why," said Little Owl.